TAKE THE PIZZA AND RUN

And Other Stories for Children about Stewardship

By Barbara DeGrote
Illustrated by Ray Martens

Augsburg Fortress ◆ Minneapolis

Contents

Take the Pizza and Run

Design: Connie Helgeson-Moen
Illustration: Ray Martens
Editors: Beth Ann Gaede and Louise Lystig

This storybook is prepared for use with the Peli-can Project, a program of stewardship education developed by the Division for Congregational Ministries, the Hunger Program of the Evangelical Lutheran Church in America, and Augsburg Fortress, Publishers. For a current listing of Peli-can resources, call or write the Peli-can Project, ELCA, 8765 West Higgins Road, Chicago, Illinois 60631, (800) 638-3522.

Scripture quotations are from The Good News Bible, Today's English Version copyright © 1966, 1971, 1976 American Bible Society. Reprinted by permission.

Take the Pizza and Run

"I was hungry and you fed me . . . ; I was a stranger and you received me in your homes" (Matthew 25:35).

It didn't take a genius to see that Robbie and Ryan had been in Sara's room again. Sara Roberts blinked twice as she scanned her room for damage. Comic books were strewn on the floor, her dresser drawers hung open, and her clothes hamper sat on top of her bed, the dirty clothes scattered across her room.

Sara stopped to listen. Something else was bothering her besides the mess. The silence. It was too quiet. Robbie and Ryan were never quiet unless they had done something wrong or were sneaking outside to . . . play ball!

Jumping over her unmade bed, Sara pushed her dresser a few inches out from the wall.

"They got it!" she screamed. "They got my glove!"

Pieces of twisted masking tape dangled where Sara had taped her glove to the back of the dresser the day before. Peeling off the tape, Sara wadded it into tight little balls and tossed them toward the wastepaper basket. Three hit the rim and one went in. This wasn't the first time Robbie and Ryan had used her glove, uninvited, but it would be the last!

Everything had been so nice and neat when it was just Sara and her mom. Nobody to share anything with, including

the bathroom. Mom had her room, and Sara had hers.

Things changed when Sara's mom married Larry. Overnight her nice, neat family of two evolved into five, not counting Larry's dog, Cuffy, and Robbie and Ryan's hamsters. It seemed like nothing belonged just to Sara anymore.

"I know," she said aloud. "I'll make a list of everything Robbie and Ryan have taken from my room and give it to Mom and Larry. They'll have to do something if I write it down for them."

Sara leaned her desk chair back on two legs and pulled out the top drawer where she kept her pencils. Flicking on her radio, Sara reached for the three red pencils she kept tucked in the right-hand corner of the top drawer. The ones with Sara Roberts stamped in gold. The ones she used only for really important assignments. In their place she found two broken crayons and a dried out marker, an obvious attempt by Robbie and Ryan to replace what they had borrowed.

"Ah-h-h!" Sara screamed, slamming her desk drawer. "Not my pencils, too!"

Sara heard the boys yelling outside as they tossed a ball back and forth. Sara wondered who was using her glove—Robbie or Ryan. It didn't matter. They were both in trouble.

Throwing open her window, Sara yelled, "Who took my glove?" at the two seven-year-olds below.

Robbie and Ryan squinted up at Sara. "We did. Want to play?" Robbie yelled back.

"Why'd you have it taped to your dresser, anyway? We had a hard time finding it!" Ryan added.

Sara stuck her head farther out the window. "That's the whole point!" she screamed louder yet. "You weren't

supposed to find it!''

"Oh-oh!'' Ryan answered, looking at Robbie. "But Robbie and I share everything. You don't have to be so . . . piggy!''

"Piggy! Piggy!'' Sara shouted back, bumping her head on the window. "It's my stuff! Mine! Stay out! And that's an order!''

Sara slammed the window and huffed her way back to her desk. It would take more than a letter to Mom and Larry to straighten out Robbie and Ryan.

"That's right folks! A free extra-large pepperoni pizza with double cheese, delivered tonight to your doorstep,'' Sara's radio blared. "Just be the sixth caller to identify this 'oldie but goodie,' and that pizza is on its way.''

Sara's hand shot up toward the on-off button but shot down again as the song began to play.

"I know that song. Larry and Mom had it sung at their wedding,'' Sara said. "Something about beginnings . . .''

"Call now! 555-2211,'' the radio announcer boomed. "One pizza just for you.''

Sara tore down the stairs to the kitchen and dialed the number.

"You're our sixth caller,'' the man's voice from the radio answered. "Go ahead.''

"Is it—'We've Only Just Begun'?'' Sara gasped into the phone, out of breath from her sprint down the stairs.

"We have our winner,'' the man announced. "No more calls, please. We have our winner. Hold on, and we'll get your name and address.''

Sara squealed into the phone. One extra-large pepperoni pizza with double cheese, and she didn't have to share. The man said so.

Hanging up the phone, Sara breezed back to her room. Never mind the borrowed glove. Never mind that her three favorite pencils were missing. Tonight she would eat an entire pizza in front of Robbie and Ryan. And even if they begged, they weren't getting any.

Sara began to throw her clothes back into her hamper. She hadn't felt so good in weeks.

◆　◆　◆

It was Larry's night to cook, which meant vegetable-something was on the menu. Larry was into vegetables, whole grains, and anything else that "kept the old machine in good working order."

"What's for supper?" Robbie asked, sniffing the air.

"Zucchini casserole. My specialty," Larry answered. "Did you kids wash up?"

"Yeah."

"Kind of."

"Kind of."

Larry turned and pointed to the bathroom, and Ryan and Robbie marched off obediently.

Sara hadn't told anybody that at 5:45 P.M. her prize-winning pizza was being delivered. It would be a surprise, and that was the way she wanted it. Sara looked at her watch. Eight minutes till show time.

Larry threw a piece of zucchini to Cuffy, who gobbled it in mid-air. Larry even had Cuffy liking vegetables.

"Sara, could you put these plates on for me? I'm just about ready," Larry asked.

Sara grabbed the plates off the counter and finished setting the table in silence. She liked Larry OK. It's just that when they were alone she never knew

what to say.

"The boys are kinda getting to you, aren't they?" Larry said. "I know they get to me sometimes, too."

Sara looked up from the table. "What do you mean?" she asked back, surprised that Larry knew what she was thinking.

"For Robbie and Ryan, whatever one has, the other has. They've always been like that. They have a hard time understanding that they need to ask to use some things. We're working on it, Sara," Larry said, kindly.

"It *is* my stuff," Sara said. "Nobody's

ever wanted to use my stuff before. I guess it's hard for me to share everything.''

"Well, you've been great about sharing your mom with me," Larry answered.

"At least you asked," Sara reminded him. "I could have said 'no.' "

"I guess I did ask," Larry laughed, "and I'm glad you said 'yes.' "

"I said 'maybe,' " Sara reminded him, smiling slightly.

Larry put the steaming casserole on the table and called the boys back.

"You're quite a girl, Sara. I'm happy that we're a family. And I'll talk to Robbie and Ryan about staying out of your room, OK?"

Sara grinned. If Larry could make a dog eat vegetables, he could make Robbie and Ryan stay out of her room. "OK," she agreed, flashing a thumbs up.

A loud rumble from the garage made Cuffy charge into the room and wait by the back door.

"There's your mom," Larry announced. "Right on time. Places everyone."

The back door slammed and Sara's mom walked in—a big pizza box balanced on her hand. "Anybody know anything about this?" she asked, placing the extra-large pepperoni pizza with double cheese down on the counter. "I met the delivery girl in the driveway. She insisted that this was ours and it had already been paid for, so I took it."

"Pizza!" Robbie yelled.

"Pizza!" Ryan echoed.

Larry removed the zucchini casserole from its place of honor. "We can have this tomorrow," he said. "I can see I'm outnumbered tonight!"

"Sara, you're the only one who doesn't look surprised," her mom said.

Sara gulped. This was not going the way she had planned. Somehow eating the whole pizza in front of her family didn't have the same appeal as it had an hour ago. Maybe some things, like pizza, belong to everybody.

"I won it on the radio," said Sara. "I was the sixth caller, and I remembered the song from your wedding. It was 'We've Only Just Begun.'"

"Cool," Robbie said. "Sara won this huge pizza. Let's eat!"

"Maybe it's hers," Ryan butted in. "Is it yours, Sara?"

"Well," Sara began, "I did win it . . . and I could eat it all by myself . . . but I won't!"

"Hurrah!" Robbie and Ryan whooped it up as they started to dig in.

"Whoa, boys," Sara's mom laughed. "Pray first!"

Twenty minutes later all that remained of the pizza was the cardboard. Sara slipped Cuffy the last bite of her last piece of crust and moaned, "I'm stuffed."

"Compliments of WRXX, your local radio call-in show!" Larry announced, using his best radio voice.

"No way!" Robbie said. "This pizza's from Sara!"

"What did I tell you, Sara?" Larry whispered. "They're shaping up already!"

Questions

1) Why was it so hard for Sara to share? Should she share everything? Why or why not?

2) What had Sara already shared with Larry, Ryan, and Robbie?

3) What things belong to your whole family? What things belong to only you?

4) What things does your family share with other people?

Activities

1) Let a pizza represent all the food eaten in the world today. Divide the pizza according to the percentages of food eaten on each of the five most populated continents.

	WORLD POPULATION	FOOD EATEN
Africa	12%	8%
Asia	58%	23%
Europe	16%	36%
North America	6%	22%
South America	8%	11%

Discuss how the people who live on the more populated continents might feel about the people who get more than their fair share of the world's food. Redivide the pizza fairly.

2) Study the food chain. Try a vegetarian meal. Discuss why eating low on the food chain is a good idea.

3) Think of someone who might enjoy sharing a meal with your family and invite him or her over.

4) Read Genesis 1:29. Think of a fruit or vegetable that begins with each letter of the alphabet. Draw letters that look like that fruit or vegetable. Thank God for giving us such wonderful variety in our food.

5) When possible, set an empty place at the table to represent the others in the world who do not share in the abundance.

6) Buy at least one item for your local foodshelf every time you go to the grocery store.

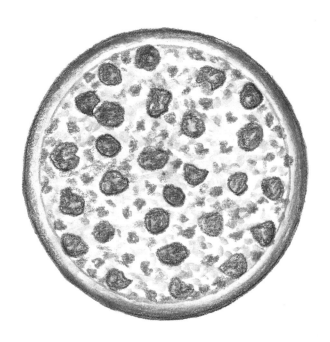

The "R" Word

"For everyone has to carry his own load" (Galatians 6:5).

Juan Moreno stared at the blinking digital clock next to his bed. The electricity had gone off during the night, and now everyone was scrambling to get ready. If he hurried, he could still make the bus.

"Get a move on, Juan," Mrs. Moreno called from the upstairs bathroom. "Michael still needs his diaper bag packed for the day-care center, and I need to iron my dress."

Juan lay on his stomach and rummaged under his bed for his new tennis shoes—the ones with the neon laces that had been his one-and-only Christmas gift. It hadn't mattered. It was all he wanted, and he knew his mother had spent a lot to get them.

"There's one," Juan said, pulling the shoe out from under a pile of stuff. "The other has to be here somewhere!"

Juan could hear the grind of the school bus engine two blocks away as it geared up Chesterhill Drive and stopped to pick up Juan's best friend, Stewie. The bus made only two stops between Stewie's and Juan's houses. Juan dug frantically to find his lost shoe. Papers, books, and a forgotten banana peel flew out from under his bed as he made one last-ditch effort.

"Juan!" Mrs. Moreno yelled. "Can you hold Michael while I . . ."

Mrs. Moreno stopped in mid-sentence as she stood in the doorway to Juan's torn-apart bedroom. "Madre mia!" she said.

10

Juan knew he was in trouble now. His mother used Spanish only when she was really mad or when she talked to Grandma.

Mrs. Moreno sighed as she plunked Michael down on the floor and finished putting the belt around her freshly ironed dress. "Juan, you have to be more careful with your things. I can't keep paying money to replace stuff that you've been careless with. Look at this room. And you know how much those shoes cost! We're going to have to talk about this later."

Juan looked down just in time to watch Michael stick part of the banana peel in his mouth.

"Yucky, Michael! Spit it out. Spit it out, Michael." Mrs. Moreno held out her hand, and Michael spit a slightly chewed blackened peel into her palm.

"Find your shoe, Juan, and I'll get your jacket. I think you can still make that bus," Mrs. Moreno yelled over her shoulder as she hurried down the hall with the squirming Michael.

Jacket!

Running down the hall, Juan scooted past the TV area. His missing shoe lay next to the empty popcorn bowl, its laces smeared with butter blobs and little pieces of dried popcorn. Juan scurried out the door, his eyes searching quickly across the yard, down along the side fence, and back across to the basketball net. There they stopped. The jacket lay in a heap on the ground, mud-spattered and wet.

"Juan!" Mrs. Moreno yelled again. "I couldn't find your . . ."

"I've got it, Mom!" Juan butted in. "It's just a little . . . ah, wet."

Mrs. Moreno stuck her head out the front door. "Wet?" she asked.

Juan took the dripping jacket from behind his back and held it out for his mom to see. "Sorry," he said. "But I found my shoe." He decided to leave out the butter blob part. It's best not to push parents too far—especially when they're late.

Mrs. Moreno sighed. "You'll have to use your sweatshirt today, Juan. There's not time to dry your jacket, and you're going to need something."

Juan squirmed inside. "Not the red sweatshirt. The one that makes me look like a stop sign. *Please* not the red sweatshirt."

Mrs. Moreno returned with Michael and the diaper bag in one hand, her briefcase and the red sweatshirt in the other, and her car keys dangling from her mouth. "You'll have to ride wif' me," she said through clenched teeth. "I think you've miffed your buf."

Juan looked up in time to see the school bus load the last kid from his block, close its doors, and rumble loudly out of sight.

◆　◆　◆

It took Juan's mother only two stop lights before she broke her silence and started in on the lecture. Juan let her words go by. He had more important things to think about, like who might recognize their slightly dented blue station wagon when it pulled up in front of his school. Wearing a red sweatshirt wasn't going to help either. Somebody was going to see him getting a ride to school with his mother. What a wimp. The day was doomed.

"I'm not made of money, Juan," Mrs. Moreno continued. "I just don't think it's

fair that I should pay for things that you lose, break, or forget somewhere. You are responsible for your own actions, and this time it's going to cost you something."

Cost! Juan's drifted attention came shooting back into the car. Cost meant money. "My money!" Juan thought, not liking the sound of where his mother's lecture was going.

"Last week it was library fines: $1.25 in overdue penalties, plus another nine dollars to replace the book that Michael scribbled in."

"That wasn't my fault!" Juan cut in. "Michael did it!"

Hearing his name, Michael smiled at Juan, while a big blob of drool oozed down his chin and onto the straps of his carseat.

"You left it out where he could get it, Juan. So it was your responsibility," Mrs. Moreno countered. "Add that to the cost of dry-cleaning your jacket—I'll never get all that mud out in the wash—I figure you owe me about 16 dollars. Does that sound fair?"

Juan gulped. "Ah . . . I don't have 16 dollars," Juan managed to sputter, trying desperately to think of a way out of this new dilemma.

"But do you think it's fair, Juan? I mean, it is your . . ."

Juan heard it coming. The "R" word. Responsibility. It wasn't a word that Juan heard kids using very much, but grown-ups sure seemed to like it.

"I mean, how would you like it if Michael wrote on my library books, and I expected you to pay for them?" Mrs. Moreno continued.

Juan couldn't think of anything to say to that. His mother had a point.

"But I still don't have 16 dollars," Juan finally answered.

"I realize that," Mrs. Moreno said, breezing into the school parking lot. "But there is a way you can pay me back anyway. I have to show a house today after school. I had planned to leave Michael at day-care an extra couple of hours. Instead, I'll drop him off at home, and you can watch him. I'll pay you the same as I pay the day-care. And then you can pay me back. Fair?" Mrs. Moreno asked again.

Parked in front of the school, Juan felt it best to agree as quickly as possibly.

"Fair," he said, opening the car door and jumping out.

"Say 'good-bye' to Juan, Michael," Mrs. Moreno said.

Juan leaned back in to tousle the baby's hair. "See you later," he said to the smiling Michael. Michael waved a slimy fist up and down in the air.

Juan jumped back out of the car, bumping his head on the doorframe. Trying to forget he looked like a stop sign, he ran toward the front door just as the five-minute warning bell began to ring.

◆　◆　◆

"What do you mean you have to babysit," Stewie whined. "You promised you'd go to the skateboard exhibition at the high school today."

"Forgot," Juan said, not wanting to get into all the details with Stewie. "Besides, my mom's making me."

"Oh!" Stewie said, suddenly sympathetic. "Well, come and watch anyway. I'm going to check out the competition and might try a few of my own tricks in the freestyle comps."

"What about Michael?" Juan said. "I'm not sure I can bring him."

But Mrs. Moreno gave the OK for Michael to go on the outing. "Just keep him in his backpack" was all she said as she handed Michael to Juan and headed off to her showing.

By the time Juan and Michael arrived, Stewie was already in the stands. The crowd was cheering wildly as a boy with a super flashy board spun around in mid-air and completed his routine.

"They're good," Stewie said, not taking his eyes off the competitors.

Michael squirmed slightly in his backpack, then put his head down and went to sleep on Juan's shoulder.

"Look at their boards," Stewie continued. "I'd never stand a chance with this piece of junk."

Stewie spun the wheels of the skateboard lying across his lap. Like Juan's neon-laced tennis shoes, Stewie's skateboard had been his only Christmas present. It was a good board. Not the best. But good.

"Get real," Juan laughed. "Your board's always been good enough for the stuff we do."

"Not anymore," Stewie sulked. "Listen. I'm going to—you know—lose my board. You know, like toss it. Maybe I can say somebody took it. If you'd stick up for me, my folks would believe me. They might even get me a new one."

Juan laughed again. "Like you want me to lie to your parents?"

"It wouldn't be lying really," Stewie argued. "I am going to lose it. I mean, it really would be lost."

Juan looked at Stewie. Stewie had never asked Juan to do anything like this before.

"I don't want to watch any more," Juan said. "I have to get Michael home anyway."

Juan watched as Stewie jumped down from the bleachers and headed toward the big steel drums near the concession stand. As the boys passed the cans, Juan heard a loud clanging noise as Stewie's board landed in the pile of empty pop cans and crumpled candy wrappers.

"Hey! My board," Stewie said, pretending to be surprised. "Somebody took my board." He whispered, "I'll let you know if I need you to back me up."

"Wait!" Juan blurted out. "You can't just trash it, Stewie."

"Why not?" Stewie shrugged. "How else am I going to get a different board?"

Juan paused. Maybe he should talk to Stewie about the "R" word, but somehow he didn't think Stewie would listen.

"You could always . . . get a job," Juan suggested, looking back to see if Michael was still asleep.

"I'm 12, remember," Stewie said, unimpressed. "Anyway, my mind's made up."

In a few seconds, Juan was standing alone with the sleeping Michael still snoring quietly from his backpack. Watching Stewie trash his skateboard reminded Juan of his mother's lecture. It wasn't fair for Stewie to expect his parents to buy him a new skateboard when he didn't take care of his old one. There had to be a better way.

Juan pulled Stewie's skateboard from the garbage can, spun its wheels a few times, tucked it under his arm, and headed for home. Stewie didn't know it, but his skateboard had just been found.

Juan laughed a little as he thought of the look on Stewie's face when his skateboard just happened to reappear tomorrow. Maybe Stewie could trade in his board for a better one or get a babysitting job. Work wasn't so bad once you got used to it, Juan thought.

Suddenly, a warm slippery something ran down the back of Juan's neck.

"Michael! Hey, Michael, don't drool on your big brother," Juan suddenly shouted. "Michael, yuck!"

16

Questions

1) Stewie threw his skateboard away. What are some other ways a person could "trash" their possessions without actually tossing them in the garbage?

2) Describe how well you take care of some of the things that belong to you.

3) Why is it easier to blame someone other than ourselves when things break or disappear?

4) Did Stewie make a good choice about his skateboard? In what other ways could Juan help Stewie show more responsibility towards his possessions?

Activities

1) Have a fix-up night at your house. Collect all broken toys, games with pieces missing, and batteries that need recharging. Spend time as a family making the old new again. Look for other things that you can fix.

2) If a child doesn't respond to a request for help around the house, "hire" another family member to do the job. The child who turned down the job is required to pay the "hired" person for doing the job for them, (for example, 25 cents to set the table, ten cents to hang up the other's backpack).

3) Psalm 24:1 says: "The world and all that is in it belong to the Lord; the earth and all who live on it are his." Talk with your class or family about owning and borrowing. Does anyone really own anything, or are we just borrowing it from the Lord? How should we treat things that are borrowed?

Family Hug

"Why won't God give me what I ask?" (Job 6:8)

Matt scrambled out of the family car, dragging his hockey mask, pads, stick, and a huge dufflebag behind him. He had two hours of ice time to practice. The Bantam tryouts were just two weeks away, and Matt wanted to be ready. He already had his new skates, and he was skating every day now, although ice time was expensive. If he made the Bantams, there would be a lot more expense for gear and travel. Matt wasn't especially worried about the cost, though. His parents had always paid for stuff like that.

"I'll pick you up at six, then," his dad said, checking their signals. "Stay here until I beep my horn. I might be a few minutes late."

"Sure thing," Matt shot back. His body might have been in the parking lot, but his brain was already in the ice arena. Moving the puck down the ice and having a clear shot at the goal was enough to live on for a week.

By 6:30 Matt had begun to worry. His dad was never this late to pick him up from practice. Something must be wrong, or he would have called. Matt peered out the semi-frosted glass into the pitch-black parking lot. Suddenly, a familiar car pulled up, and Matt heard two short blasts that signaled him to come on out.

"Dad! Where were you? I almost called Mom. Practice has been over for half an hour. I thought you said a few . . ."

Matt stopped shoving his gear into the backseat of the car and stared at his dad's face. Something was wrong all right.

"It's OK, Matt," Mr. DeLaney said. "I just got some bad news. Hop in, and I'll explain when we get home."

Twenty minutes later, Matt and his dad turned off the main road and headed down the familiar country drive to their home.

"What do you mean, they're closing?" Matt heard his mother whisper to Dad in the kitchen as he hung up his stuff.

"Closing. Transferring a few into the main office, but the rest of us—well, we got our notice," Matt's dad replied.

Matt heard his parents whisper something about "after dinner" but couldn't make out enough of the words to make sense of anything. All he knew was that something had changed, and both Dad and Mom seemed worried about it.

"I was let go today," Mr. DeLaney announced to his startled family as he cleared the supper dishes.

"You mean fired?" Ali, Matt's younger sister, asked. "Did you do something bad, Daddy?"

Mr. DeLaney looked surprised and then smiled a little. "No, honey, I didn't do anything bad. Our office is going out of business, and most of us have to find new jobs."

"Oh," Ali said. "Well, that's OK then. Can I go play?"

Mr. DeLaney gave her a hug. "Sure, honey, go and play."

But Matt knew it was not OK. Without their dad's job, where would they get the money to pay for stuff like clothes or cars or . . . hockey.

"Matt?" Mrs. DeLaney said. "Are you worried, honey? Do you want to talk to Dad and me?"

Matt didn't want to make his dad feel any worse than he did, but he needed to know. "How will we live?" he blurted out. "If we don't have any money, how can we buy . . . ," Matt paused and didn't finish his sentence.

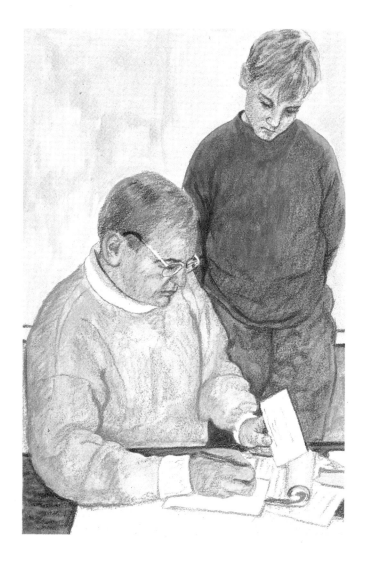

"Is that all our money?" Matt finally asked. "What are you doing with it?"

Mr. DeLaney explained that the family would be on a new budget or plan for how they spend their money. Each envelope showed how much they could spend that month on different things. "It helps us set limits, Matt, so we don't spend more than we have."

Matt looked at the envelopes marked food, clothes, car, medical, house, church, and odds and ends. There wasn't anything that said "hockey lessons." "What about hockey lessons?" he asked. "And what about the Bantams?"

"We're all giving things up, Matt. I wish you didn't have to, too. Ali will be staying with me instead of going to preschool for a while. We'll be selling one of our cars, and your mom is going to take the bus to work. I'm dropping my membership at the health club. "We'll make it work, Matt. But we all have to help."

Matt looked down again at the seven envelopes lying on the table. "What about church? We don't owe the church money. That's free."

Mr. DeLaney took the envelope marked "church" and laid it at the top of the pile. "This money is a gift back to God. God never stops giving us gifts, so we don't want to stop giving to God either."

Matt was silent for a long time. If there wasn't money for hockey, there shouldn't be money for gifts either—even to God.

Matt smiled just because he thought it would make his dad feel better. But inside, he wasn't smiling at all. Things were going to change all right. What if his dad didn't get a new job? What if he never got to take hockey lessons again? What if. . . ?

Mr. DeLaney moved over next to Matt and his mom. "We've got some money put aside, and the company is giving us all a little until we find other jobs. Your mother still has her job at the clinic. We'll have enough, Matt, but we may have to make some changes until I'm back on my feet again."

That night Matt watched as his parents worked on their pile of bills. When they finished, his parents took out seven envelopes and began to put money into each one.

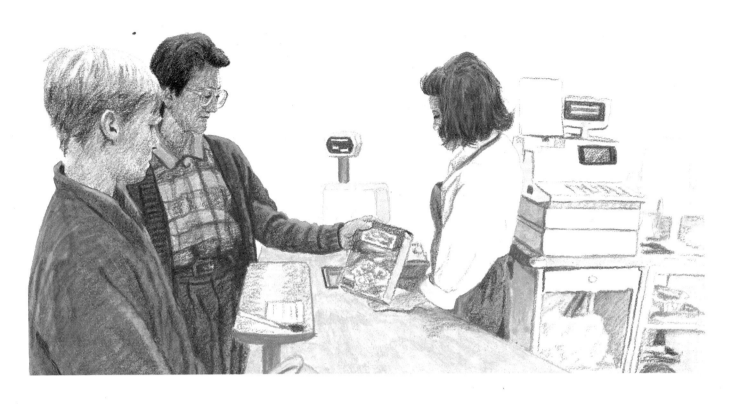

◆ ◆ ◆

"Can I have a treat?" Ali asked, as Mrs. DeLaney pushed the grocery cart up the produce aisle of their grocery store.

"No, honey. But we can make some cookies when we get home, if you want," Mrs. DeLaney suggested as she threw a bag of carrots in the cart.

Matt had noticed his mother wasn't buying some of the more convenient frozen stuff they usually counted on for busy nights. Instead she bought "real food," as she liked to call it. Rice, potatoes, vegetables, fruit. Last night they had even made their own pizza. It tasted good, Matt thought, and he liked that the family was staying home together more than usual. If it hadn't been for hockey, cutting back wouldn't seem so terrible.

The cashier rang up the groceries and then began to deduct the coupons Matt's mom had clipped from that week's paper. "That's $104.82."

Mrs. DeLaney pulled out five twenty-dollar bills from her wallet and fished out some ones from her coin purse.

Matt watched, surprised at the high total. A hundred dollars. "Mom," he whispered, "can we afford all this?"

Mrs. DeLaney turned a slight shade of pink. "Thank you," she told the cashier. "We'll drive up."

In the car, Mrs. DeLaney turned to Matt and explained. "That was embarrassing, Matt. Of course we can afford food. We have a budget, remember! You don't need to worry about food. Dad and I have this under control."

Mrs. DeLaney turned onto the freeway. As they passed a speed limit sign she turned to Matt again.

"I'm sorry, Matt," she said. "I know this isn't easy for you. But you've been really good about the hockey lessons, and Dad and I have been thinking about a way that maybe you can play again."

Matt squirmed in his seat. "It's just that I don't like it when I want something, and I can't have it," he said, honestly.

Matt's mom pointed to the speed limit sign they just passed. "See that sign, Matt?"

Matt nodded, wondering what speed limit signs had to do with hockey and money.

"Almost everything has limits, Matt. If we break the speed limit, we put ourselves in danger of a serious accident," Mrs. DeLaney explained.

Matt nodded, pretending to understand.

"The same goes with our money. All people have spending limits. If we go over our limit, we put ourselves in a serious situation, too. No matter how much money you make, there will always be something else you want."

Matt shook his head a little. "But hockey is important to me."

The light changed to green, and Matt's mom turned a sharp right down Beacon Street instead of taking their usual route. "When I was your age, nothing was more important to me than swimming faster than anybody else," Mrs. DeLaney said with a smile. "But that's before someone told me that swimming, like everything else, was a gift, not something I owned. See, Matt, Dad and I may earn our money. We may think it's all ours, but it really isn't."

"It's not? But if you earned it . . ." Matt argued back a little.

"Right. But it is God's gifts that allow us to work at all. God gives us everything—even the ability to make a good salary. God has given us so much, and it has made us very comfortable. But Dad's losing his job has made us see things a little differently now."

"What do you mean?" Matt asked.

"The purpose of God's gift, Matt, was not to make us comfortable, but to make us generous. Look around us, Matt," Mrs. DeLaney said, as they drove through a poorer section of town. "Even though Dad lost his job and money is tight, we still have more than enough to meet our needs." Mrs. DeLaney looked out the window again. "I'm not going to complain that I have to take the bus to work when most of these people have no car at all. Everyone has limits, Matt."

Matt didn't really like the word "limits," but he was beginning to understand it a little better.

"But, Matt?" Mrs. DeLaney asked.

"Yeah."

"There are two things that have no limits," Mrs. DeLaney said.

"What's that?"

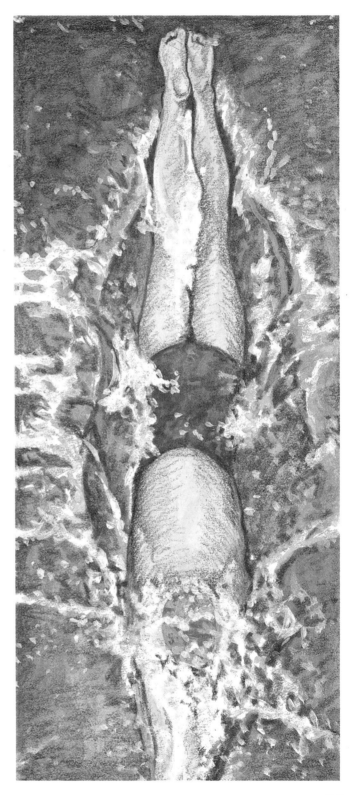

"How much God loves you, and how much your dad and I love you and Ali. There's no limit on love, Matt."

Matt smiled to himself. "That's good, I guess, huh?"

Mrs. DeLaney smiled back. "That's very good, Matt."

◆　◆　◆

Mr. DeLaney was just hanging up the phone when the rest of the family came through the back door, lugging the groceries.

"Where do you want all this extra toilet paper?" Matt asked as he began to unload groceries onto the kitchen counter.

"Twelve rolls?" Mr. DeLaney laughed.

"It was on sale."

Mr. DeLaney just kept laughing, as if 12 rolls of toilet paper was the funniest thing he'd ever seen.

"Ron," Mrs. DeLaney stopped her sorting. "What's wrong. I mean—what's happened. Something's happened, Ron. Tell me."

To Matt and Ali's surprise, Mr. DeLaney swept up his wife and Ali with one arm and wrestled Matt into the tight family circle with the other arm.

"Family hug! Family hug!" Ali yelled, squeezing her dad around the neck until his face turned bright red.

"OK, OK!" Mr. DeLaney declared. "I'll tell you. That was the Stevens Agency on 42nd Street. They heard the company was closing, and they have room to take a new partner—part-time for awhile. It's not as big a job as I had, but they said maybe down the road it could open up."

"Oh, Ron! That's great," Mrs. DeLaney said, hugging her husband again. "They know a good thing when they see it."

"Did Daddy get a new job?" Ali asked.

"I did at that, sweetie," Mr. DeLaney answered.

"Good. Can I go play now?" Ali asked and left to finish the fort she had started earlier in the family room.

"Hey! Matt!" Mr. DeLaney said, drawing his son closer for another hug. "Grab your stuff. We've got some work to do."

"What stuff?" Matt asked, wondering if there were some more groceries left in the car.

"Your hockey stuff. Your dear old dad's gonna coach you himself. There's a great rink down at Lester Park that hardly anyone uses," Mr. DeLaney laughed. "We may not be able to swing the Bantam league this year, but the city rec team is looking for a great goalie, and I think I just found their man. What do you say?"

Matt felt his jaw drop, and then he let out a whoop. His dad was a great skater, at least he used to be before he got so busy. And the rec team might not be the best team in town, but they played once during the week and twice on weekends.

"I say, 'Great!'" Matt yelled, grabbing his gear and heading for the car. "I say, 'Great!'"

Questions

1) Where does your family get its money? What would happen if someone in your family lost his or her job?

2) Tell about two of your favorite possessions. Which one possession would you choose if you could have only one? Could you live without either of them?

3) What did Matt's mother mean when she said, "We have more than enough"?

4) What good things happened to Matt's family because they had to cut back on spending?

5) Why is it important to give an offering, especially when you do not have much money to spend or when you would rather spend the money on something else?

Activities

1) Going on a family trip or even on a morning of garage sales can give children the chance to make wise decisions about their money. Start a Saturday with one dollar for each person. Each person decides on his or her own purchases, but when the one dollar is gone, that's it. Sometimes the dollar won't be spent, and then it can be saved for another time. Sometimes children will pool their money to get a larger item. In either case, the decisions are theirs and they won't be asking, "Can I have this?" They will learn to set their own limits.

2) Have children make a money mural to educate the congregation about how their regular offering is used for ministry.

3) Hold your own garage sale. Plan a lemonade and popcorn stand to be run by children. Lend the children money up front for supplies. Help them figure their profits and give ten percent to the church as a special offering. Remember to give ten percent from the garage sale earnings, too.

When a Pelican Follows You Home

"Your Father in heaven knows you need all these things" (Matthew 6:32).

Waiting on the pier for CJ was not Stephie Engles' favorite pastime. CJ, Stephie's older brother and her only way home, was late as usual. It seemed to Stephie that she spent most of her life waiting—waiting for rides, waiting in line for lunch, or just waiting to grow up.

Today she was tired of waiting, and her mood matched the overcast sky that melted into the gray-blue of the ocean waves. Turning to check the parking lot once more for CJ's red scooter, Stephie walked down the wooden walkway and stared off at the waves crashing over the coral reef that gave Bathtub Bay its name.

At least the pelicans are enjoying themselves, she thought, watching a trio of birds swoop down across the beach and out over the growing pull of the tide. Stephie watched as the biggest bird dove for the water and flew off, his pouch full of tasty morsels.

Now that's more like it, Stephie continued her daydreams. *Pelicans don't wait for anything. If they see something they want, they just dive down and get it. They can take all they want.*

It wasn't just waiting for CJ that put Stephie in such a stormy mood. It had more to do with the fact that Brenda Gerchenilli had worn the most awesome

outfit to school. It's not that Stephie was jealous of Brenda. Not really. But Brenda, just like the pelicans, always got what she wanted. No waiting until she had saved enough or was old enough or anything. Brenda had it all.

CJ whistled from the pier steps, and Stephie gathered up her stuff for the ride home.

"Sorry I took so long," CJ apologized. "I had to wait for Mr. Thao to correct my test."

Stephie jumped on the back of CJ's scooter, put on her helmet, and grabbed hold. CJ was well known for his jerky starts, and so with two little hiccups his scooter jumped into first gear and took off.

Crossing over the bay bridge, Stephie nudged CJ in the ribs. "Look, over there!" she said, pointing over the metal girders where a single pelican flew parallel with their scooter. "What a crazy bird. It's like he wants to race or something."

Stephie watched the big bird glide smoothly in the air, almost without effort. Stephie let go of CJ long enough to wiggle a few fingers in greeting. The bird looked briefly at Stephie, tipped to its side, and

soared off toward a nearby dock post, leaving Stephie with the feeling that the bird knew her.

That's ridiculous. All pelicans look the same. But all the way home Stephie had the feeling that the pelican had been trying to tell her something. Something about Bathtub Bay? Something about . . . Stephie didn't know. It was strange.

CJ steered the scooter into the drive of their melon-colored rambler with the basketball hoop over the garage, parked his scooter next to the garbage cans, grabbed a basketball, and attempted a left hand hook. The ball skidded off toward the rock garden.

"Did you see that crazy bird?" Stephie asked. "The one that was following us?"

"You know pelicans like to play," CJ said, tossing the ball toward the hoop again. "Maybe it followed you home!"

Stephie took a quick look around. "I wouldn't mind being one of those," she said.

CJ stopped shooting and laughed. "One of what? A basketball? A palm tree?" CJ's shot connected, the ball swishing the net.

"No, a pelican."

"I don't know, Stephie. They get terrible double chins when they get older," CJ teased.

"Seriously. Anytime pelicans want something, they just grab it and run. Take what they want, and nobody says they have to wait. I could go for that kind of life-style."

"Right!" CJ snorted. "Well, you better like fish. Besides, pelicans don't take what they want."

"They don't?"

"No way," CJ said. "They only take what they need. Ever see a fat pelican?"

"No," Stephie admitted.

"So, I proved my point," CJ snorted, swishing another basket. "Anything else you care to discuss with the great and mighty CJ?"

"You need a shower," Stephie retorted, trying to put her brother in his place.

"Yes, but do I want one, that is the question," CJ stopped dribbling. "Needs and wants, my dear Stephanie."

Stephie went into the house, grabbed the mail off the counter, and sorted through it.

This looks interesting, she thought, as she paged through a mail order catalog that had just arrived. Something on every

page called out to Stephie, screaming, "You need me! You want me! You have to have me!"

"I can't afford you," Stephie called back silently. All this "needs and wants" stuff was getting too confusing. Why did she always want to buy everything she liked anyway? "Liking doesn't mean I have to buy it," Stephie said to herself sternly. "Get a grip, Engles."

Stephie jumped up as a dark-haired woman entered the kitchen. "Hello, I . . ." Stephie stammered.

"Is that you, Stephie?" Mrs. Engles called from a back room. "We're just going through some old clothes." Her mother's voice now could be heard behind a large box that covered her face. Only her legs stuck out below as she entered the kitchen and hefted the clothes onto the table.

"This is Mrs. Menerez, Stephie. She volunteers at Agape House, the clothes closet down at church. They had a lot of clothes go out when school started, so we're collecting again. I'm sure they could use some things in your size. Have anything you can part with?" Mrs. Engles asked as she began to separate shirts from pants.

"Sure!" Stephie said. "As long as you order something new for me to replace them," and she waved the catalog in the air.

An embarrassed look crossed her mother's face. "I was thinking of things you had outgrown, Stephie. I'll come down later, Lucinda, and help sort these for size. Maybe CJ will help carry these to your car."

Stephie gulped a little gulp. She paged through the catalog one final time before tossing it in the nearby garbage. She said, "I want it, but I don't need it."

Scurrying outside Stephie yelled, "Mom! Give me 10 minutes, and I'll meet you down at the church. I have a lot of stuff to clean out, too."

Mrs. Engles suddenly pointed to the sky. "Isn't that strange to see a pelican so far inland?"

"Hey, Stephie!" CJ said, suddenly. "There's that crazy bird again."

Off toward the bay road, a pelican lifted off, its wings making a circular motion in front of its face.

"Hey, Steph. I think it's clapping for you," CJ mused. "Leave it to Steph to bring home a pelican."

Stephie watched as the bird circled her house and followed the warm breezes back to Bathtub Bay without a sound.

Questions

1) What did Brenda Gerchenilli have that Stephie wanted?

2) What does "having it all" mean? Can anybody ever "have it all"?

3) Does everybody have what they need? Who in the story did not have what they needed?

4) Why did the pelican clap its wings at the end of the story?

Activities

1) On the next visit to a shopping center, practice saying, "I like that," instead of "I want that."

2) Make a list of everything you need to live. Go back over your list and decide which of your "needs" are really "wants."

3) Brainstorm 10 ways to have fun and not spend any money. Choose three from your list and do them during vacation.